P9-DVO-224

By Wanda Coven

Illustrated by Priscilla Burris

LITTLE SIMON
New York London Toronto Sydney New Delhi

This book is a work of fiction. Any references to historical events, real people, or real places are used fictitiously. Other names, characters, places, and events are products of the author's imagination, and any resemblance to actual events or places or persons, living or dead, is entirely coincidental.

LITTLE SIMON
An imprint of Simon & Schuster Children's Publishing Division
1230 Avenue of the Americas, New York, New York 10020

Manufactured in the United States of America 1112 FFG
First Edition 10 9 8 7 6 5 4 3 2 1
Library of Congress Cataloging-in-Publication Data
Coven, Wanda.
Heidi Heckelbeck has a secret admirer / by Wanda Coven ; illustrated by Priscilla Burris. — 1st ed.
p. cm.
Summary: When Heidi is paired with Stanley, her worst enemy's best friend, for the Brewster Science Fair and she suddenly starts getting notes from a secret admirer, she tries to use magic to discover the note-writer's identity.
ISBN 978-1-4424-4174-3 (pbk. : alk. paper) — ISBN 978-1-4424-4175-0 (hardcover : alk. paper) — ISBN 978-1-4424-4176-7 (ebook)
[1. Science projects—Fiction. 2. Science fairs—Fiction. 3. Interpersonal relations—Fiction. 4. Schools—Fiction. 5. Witches—Fiction.] I. Burris, Priscilla, ill. II. Title.
PZ7.C83392Hf 2012
[Fic]—dc23
2011027868

CONTENTS

HOWDY, PARTNER!

Heidi Heckelbeck couldn't wait for the Brewster second-grade science fair. Science experiments were the next best thing to mixing magic potions.

"We find out our science partners today," said Heidi as she and Bruce Bickerson bounced along in their seat at the back of the school bus. "I hope I don't get Melanie Maplethorpe."

"Same here," Bruce said. "I wouldn't want to get her best friend, Stanley Stonewrecker, either."

"Make a fist for good luck," said Heidi.

They both made a fist.

"Pound it," said Heidi.

Bruce pounded his knuckles with Heidi's.

But it didn't seem to do any good.

When their teacher, Mrs. Welli, announced science partners, Heidi got Stanley and Bruce got Melanie.

"Poor thing," said Lucy Lancaster, who had gotten Charlie Chen.

"You're lucky you got Charlie," said Heidi. "He's nice AND smart."

Mrs. Welli asked everyone to sit with his or her partner. Heidi didn't

budge. *I'd rather sit next to an egg-salad sandwich than Stanley Stonewrecker,* she thought. Stanley set his chair next to Heidi's and sat down. Heidi wanted to stick her tongue out at him, but she didn't.

"Now it's time to pick a science experiment," said Mrs. Welli. "I have a list to choose from—or you can come up with your own."

She handed a stack of papers to Melanie to pass out.

"You have two days to choose an experiment," Mrs. Welli said. "The science fair is the following Saturday. Be ready to show your experiment to the judges. You'll also need to explain what happened and why on note cards."

Melanie dropped the list of science experiments on Heidi's desk.

"I'll bet you were behind all this, weren't you?" asked Melanie.

"Behind all what?" asked Heidi.

"Behind you getting my best friend for a partner and me getting your ding-dong friend," Melanie said.

"I'd say it pretty much stinks for all of us," said Heidi.

"Well, at least for once we agree on something," said Melanie.

Heidi

MOTHBALLS

The next day in class Heidi and Stanley flipped through the list of science experiments.

"How about a volcano?" suggested Heidi.

"That sounds cool," Stanley said. "Let's do it."

Well, that was easy, thought Heidi. She began to write "volcano" on a piece of paper to give Mrs. Welli.

Then Melanie raised her hand.

"Yes, Melanie?" said Mrs. Welli.

"Bruce and I would like to make a volcano for the science fair," said Melanie. She had overheard Heidi and Stanley talking!

"Uh . . . we *do*?" questioned Bruce.

"I thought we were going to make a shoe-box maze."

Melanie elbowed Bruce. "Play along, dum-dum," she whispered.

"Okay," Mrs. Welli said. "I'll put you down for a volcano."

Melanie turned around and made a mean face at Heidi.

Heidi pounded her fist on the desk.

"Shush," Stanley said. "We'll get in trouble."

"But she stole our idea!" said Heidi.

"We'll just have to come up with something better," said Stanley.

"Like what?" Heidi asked.

"I dunno," said Stanley. "Let's take another look."

Stanley flipped through a few

more experiments. He found a magic ketchup and an exploding lunch bag project. But nothing sounded as good as a volcano. Then Stanley remembered something he'd seen on TV.

"How about dancing mothballs?" said Stanley. "Mothballs dance when you add water and other stuff to them."

Heidi knew all about mothballs. Her grandma Mabel stored her woolens with mothballs every summer to keep away the moths. Heidi remembered how some of her grandma's sweaters would smell like mothballs even after they were no longer stored with them.

"I guess so," Heidi said.

Stanley raised his hand.

"Heidi and I would like to do dancing mothballs," said Stanley.

"Very good," said Mrs. Welli, writing it down.

"So now what?" Heidi asked.

"We need to learn more about our experiment," said Stanley.

"My dad's a soda-pop scientist," Heidi said. "Maybe he can help us. Do you want to come over after school?"

"Sure," said Stanley.

Whoa, I can't believe I just asked Stanley Stonewrecker to come over to my house, thought Heidi.

Well, it wasn't like this made him her friend or anything.

RAISINS

Ding-dong!

"I'll get it!" said Heidi as she thundered down the stairs.

Heidi met her mom and little brother, Henry, in the front hall.

"Who is it?" asked Henry.

Heidi put a finger to her lips and

whispered, "Shh . . . It's Stanley."

"SMELL-A-NIE'S Stanley?" asked Henry.

"*Shush!* He's going to hear you," Heidi whispered.

"But what's he doing here?" asked Henry.

"The two of us are working on a science project," whispered Heidi.

Ding-dong!

"Coming!" Heidi called.

"And you picked Stanley?" asked Henry.

"Of course not!" Heidi whispered loudly. "My TEACHER picked him."

"Yikes!" whispered Henry as Mom scooted him away from the door.

Heidi brought Stanley into the kitchen. "Stanley, this is my mom and my little brother, Henry," she said.

"Hi, Stanley," said Mom. "Would you like a Rice Krispies bar?"

Stanley said yes and helped himself

to one. He saw Henry pull a Candy Pop from a kitchen drawer. Henry tore off the wrapper and popped the candy into his mouth.

"That better not be the last one," Heidi said.

"It's not," said Henry. "We have five left."

"What flavors?" asked Heidi.

"Coconut," said Henry.

"What else?" Heidi asked.

Henry peeked in the candy drawer.

"More coconut," he said.

"What happened to all the grape ones?" Heidi asked.

"Maybe they got stolen," said Henry.

"Is the thief, by any chance, named HENRY?" asked Heidi.

Henry pulled the Candy Pop out of

his mouth, followed by a slimy trail of purple spit. "Want the rest of this one?" he asked.

"That's gross," Heidi said.

Henry shrugged.

Just then the back door banged open. Mr. Heckelbeck was home! He walked in and set a bag of groceries on the counter.

"The gang's all here!" said Dad cheerfully.

He introduced himself to Stanley.

"We're partners in the science fair,"

said Heidi as Dad kissed the top of her head.

"Our project is dancing mothballs," said Stanley.

"Need some help?" Dad asked.

"Yeah!" said Heidi.

"Definitely," said Stanley.

"Okay, here's what you'll need," said Dad.

Heidi got a sheet of paper and a

pencil from the kitchen desk. "Ready," she said.

"You'll need water, vinegar, baking soda, and mothballs," Dad said.

Heidi wrote everything down.

"It works with raisins, too," said Dad.

"Ooh! Let's use raisins!" said Heidi.

Stanley agreed.

Heidi wanted to do the experiment right away, but Dad had to work on a new cola.

“Let’s meet here tomorrow after school,” Dad suggested. “We’ll run the experiment from my home lab.”

“Sounds like a plan!” Heidi said. “I’ll get what we need for the experiment. Stanley, you can gather the note cards and art supplies for our poster.”

Dad held his hand in the air, and Heidi and Stanley high-fived it.

So far, so good, Heidi thought.

STINKBUG

The next morning Heidi rounded up everything they would need for the science experiment. She found an empty fishbowl in the kitchen cupboard. It was round and fat like a globe. *This will be perfect to show off our dancing raisins,* thought Heidi.

She took a big box of raisins from the pantry as well as the baking soda and vinegar. Heidi put all the items in a brown paper bag and kept it in the kitchen.

Heidi grabbed a bagel and ran to the bus stop with Henry. Today was the deadline to choose a science experiment for the fair. She wanted to find out what Lucy and Charlie had picked for their project. Heidi caught up with Lucy just before lunchtime.

"What are you and Charlie doing for the science fair?" Heidi asked.

"We're going to build a lemon battery that will light a Christmas tree bulb," said Lucy.

"A two-year-old could do THAT!"

said Melanie, who was listening in as usual. "You should call it 'Lemon Batteries for Babies.'"

"Mrs. Welli said our project was the hardest one of all," Lucy said.

"Who CARES?" said Melanie. "A volcano is WAY cooler than a battery made out of fruit. We're going to win, for sure."

Then Melanie did her famous twirl and walked off.

"What a stinkbug," said Heidi.

"You're not kidding," Lucy said. "How's it going with Stanley?"

"Okay so far," said Heidi as she reached into her cubby to grab her lunch bag.

"Wait—what's this?" Heidi asked. She stooped down to get a better look in her cubby.

Heidi pulled a bundle of grape Candy Pops from her cubby. The sticks were tied with a purple ribbon.

"These are my favorite!" said Heidi.

"I wonder where they came from," Lucy said.

"It must be Henry," said Heidi. "Yesterday, Henry ate the last grape Candy Pop, and I got really mad."

On the way to the cafeteria Heidi spied Henry in the school bus line. She waved the Candy Pops in Henry's face.

"Did you put these in my cubby?" Heidi asked.

"Why would *I* do that?" asked Henry.

"To be nice?" Heidi suggested.

"I'm not THAT nice," said Henry. "But can I have one?"

"In your dreams, bud," Heidi said, and she and Lucy continued down the hall.

In the cafeteria Lucy got in the hot-lunch line with Bruce. Heidi sat down with Charlie. They pulled out their sandwiches and water bottles.

"Want an oatmeal chocolate chip cookie?" Charlie asked. "I've got an extra."

"Sure," said Heidi.

Charlie handed her the cookie.

Then Lucy and Bruce set down their trays.

"It'll be tough to win the science fair," said Bruce. "All the second-grade classes in Brewster will be in it."

"What are YOU worried about?"

Lucy asked Bruce. "You're the smartest scientist in the whole school!"

"Probably the whole state," said Charlie.

"Probably the whole universe," said Heidi.

"Thanks, guys," Bruce said. "But

it's not me I'm worried about. It's Melanie. I'm afraid that she's going to mess things up."

"I know what you mean," Heidi said.

They ate the rest of their lunch in silence.

BUBBLES!

Mr. Heckelbeck's home laboratory had a kitchen and a library with bookcases from floor to ceiling. In the middle of the room was an island with a marble top and another sink on one side. This is where Heidi and Stanley set up their experiment.

Heidi's dad gave them each a white lab coat. Heidi set the supplies from the shopping bag on the island.

"Let's get started!" said Dad. "We need two quarts of water."

Dad handed a two-quart measuring

cup to Stanley. Stanley went to the sink and filled it with water. With Dad's help, he poured the water into the fishbowl.

"We need two-thirds of a cup of white vinegar," Dad said, pointing to

a red line on the measuring cup.

Heidi carefully poured the vinegar into the cup. The smell reminded her of dyeing Easter eggs. Then she poured the vinegar into the bowl.

"One tablespoon of baking soda," said Dad.

Stanley scooped a tablespoon of baking soda and smoothed it off with his finger. Then he dumped it into the bowl.

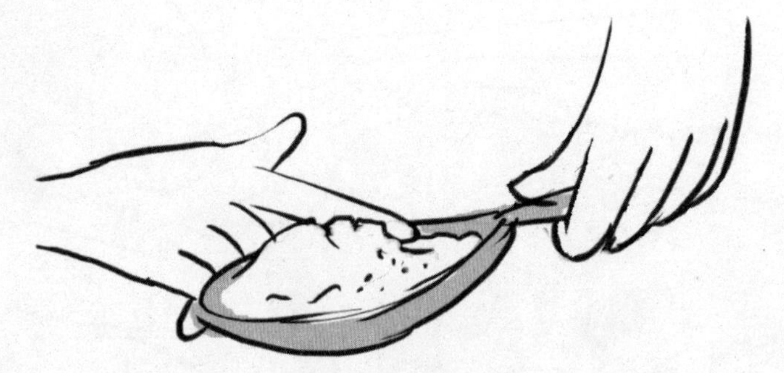

"Now for the raisins," said Dad.

Heidi dropped five raisins into the bowl.

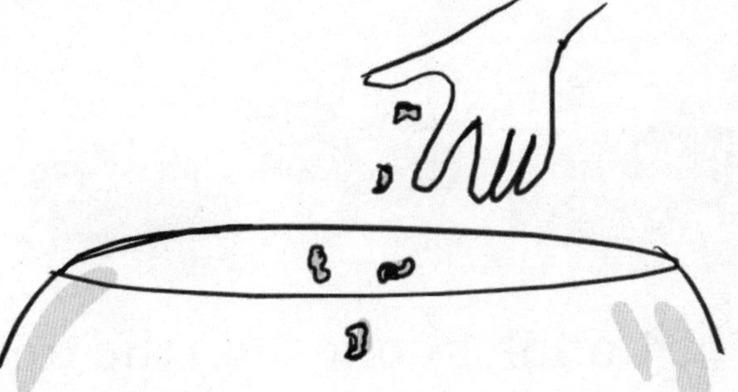

"It'll take a few minutes for the raisins to dance," said Dad.

"Why?" asked Heidi.

"Because something that's called a 'chemical reaction' is happening in the fishbowl," he said. "When you mix vinegar and baking soda, they make a gas called carbon dioxide—

that's what the bubbles actually are."

Heidi and Stanley watched bubbles form on the ridges of the raisins.

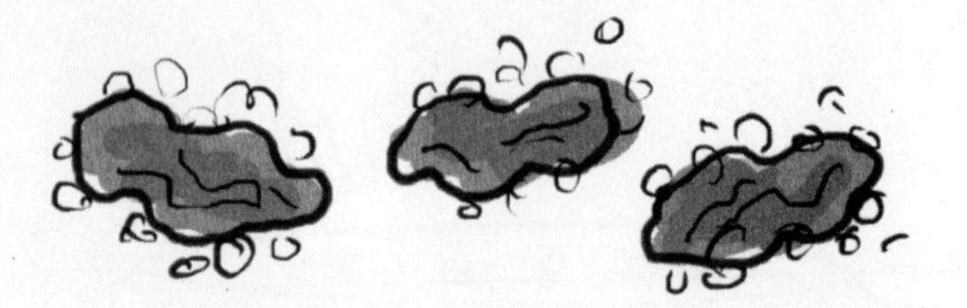

"The bubbles collect on the raisins and make them rise to the surface. When they get to the top, the bubbles pop and the raisins fall back to the bottom. Then it starts over again."

"There goes one!" said Heidi.

"There goes another!" said Stanley.

"Dad, can we add color to the water?" Heidi asked.

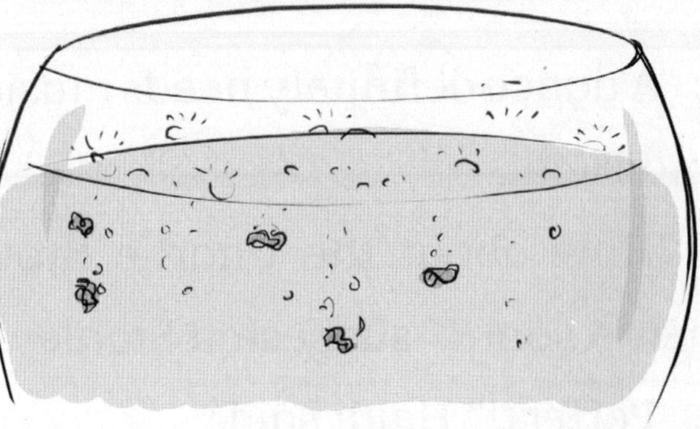

"Great idea," said Dad. He opened a drawer and pulled out a tray of food coloring.

"How about purple?" asked Heidi.

Stanley agreed, and Mr. Heckelbeck added a few drops of food coloring. The water turned a lovely shade of light purple.

"What if we added music?" said Stanley.

"A dance definitely needs music!" said Heidi.

"How about the Charlie Brown theme song?" suggested Stanley.

"Perfect!" Heidi said.

"I'll bring my dad's portable music player to the science fair," said Stanley.

"Cool," said Heidi. And then she had a thought: *Maybe the science fair won't be so bad after all.*

Heidi

The next week of school flew by. Before they knew it, the science fair was a day away! Heidi was so excited that it was hard to concentrate on anything else.

"Math books, everyone!" Mrs. Welli said.

Heidi opened her desk and found, on top of her math book, a blank piece of paper with a happy-face border. The paper was crinkly in the middle, like it had been wet. Heidi sniffed it.

The paper smelled like lemons. It had a folded note attached to it with a paper clip. Heidi undid the paper clip.

A few scratch-'n'-sniff candy stickers floated to the bottom of her desk. *Can this be from my secret admirer?* wondered Heidi. Then she unfolded the note and read it.

"Hei-di!" called Mrs. Welli. "Kindly close your desk and pay attention."

Heidi shoved the note, the stickers, and the piece of paper inside her math book and closed the lid of her desk. Then she tried to work on double-digit subtraction, but she couldn't stop thinking about the note. *Who can it be from? Maybe it's Charlie Chen. Charlie's working on a lemon battery,*

and the paper smells like lemons. Plus Charlie gave me a cookie yesterday. It HAS to be Charlie!

During silent reading Heidi took her secret message—and a book—to the reading corner. She switched on a lamp and held the paper to the light.

The message said:

You're as sweet
as a sugar beet!

From,
Your Secret
Admirer

PS: I'm not a poet,
and I know it.

Heidi quickly stuck the paper back inside her book and sat in the Comfy Chair. *I never knew Charlie liked me,* thought Heidi. *I'll have to thank him for all the cool stuff.*

In art Heidi tapped Charlie on the shoulder. He was molding a swan out of clay.

"I really liked your poem," said Heidi.

Charlie looked puzzled. "What are you talking about?" he asked.

"Didn't you leave a poem and stickers in my desk?" Heidi asked.

Charlie's cheeks began to turn red. "Huh?" he asked.

"Oh, uh, never mind," Heidi said. "Gotta go."

Heidi returned to her seat. *If Charlie isn't my secret admirer, then who can it be?*

There was one sure way to find out. . . .

BOOK

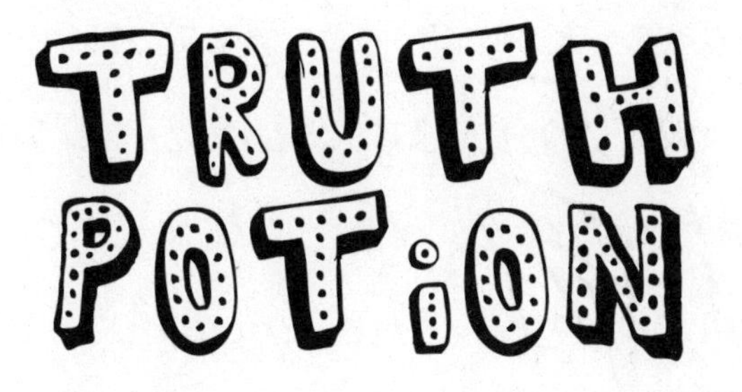

Heidi pulled her *Book of Spells* out from under the bed. She opened to a chapter called "Truth Potions." *Here we go,* she thought. Heidi read a spell:

Have you been getting candy, notes, and gifts from a mysterious person? Are you the kind of witch who will go bonkers until you know who it is? Now you can remove the mask from your secret admirer with this simple spell.

Ingredients:

1 stick of peppermint gum
1 cup of cold water
2 drops of green food coloring

This spell must be cast in the presence of your secret admirer.

Hmm, Heidi thought. *My secret admirer has to be someone at school.*

I'll be with all my classmates on the day of the science fair—that should do the trick! Heidi looked at the next step.

Mix the ingredients in a bowl. Hold your Witches of Westwick medallion in one hand. Place your other hand over the mix and chant the following words:

ALACAZABRA!
ALACAZOO!
FIND OUT WHO
IS ADMIRING YOU!

Watch the name of your secret admirer appear in the potion.

This will be a breeze, thought Heidi. *I already have a pack of peppermint gum, and I can get water at school. All I need is green food coloring and a bowl.*

Heidi crept downstairs. She listened to make sure that no one was in the kitchen. She heard music coming from the study. *Mom must be working on her jewelry,* thought Heidi. Her mom had her own jewelry business.

Heidi tiptoed into the pantry and snooped through the baking supplies. She found a box of food coloring

and peeked inside. The green was missing. *Dad must have used it up on St. Patrick's Day,* thought Heidi. He had made green pancakes and green smoothies for breakfast. *Now what am I going to do?* she wondered.

Dad had food coloring in his lab, but his lab was off-limits. *Maybe I can mix colors like Mr. Doodlebee showed us in art,* thought Heidi. She set a small container on the counter and squirted yellow food coloring into it. She added two squirts of blue. Then she stirred it with her finger. The colors swirled into a beautiful shade of emerald green. *Perfect!*

Heidi snapped the lid back on and grabbed a plastic bowl and a spoon from the kitchen. Then she

snuck upstairs to her room and put everything into her backpack. *Wait! I almost forgot,* Heidi thought. She grabbed a stick of peppermint gum from her desk and dropped it into her backpack too.

Now I will find out who likes me once and for all!

On the day of the science fair Heidi carried her fishbowl into the Brewster Elementary gym. Her spell ingredients were safely hidden in her backpack. She was wearing her Witches of Westwick medallion, but it was tucked underneath her shirt. Dad carried the

rest of Heidi's science experiment supplies in a shopping bag, and Mom held Henry's hand as she chatted with Aunt Trudy. Aunt Trudy rarely missed a family event.

A banner on the gym wall welcomed everyone. Tables with white tablecloths had been set up all around the room. The judges' table sat on a raised platform. The judges were Brewster's mayor, Lou Billings, and the editor of

Science Time! magazine, Clyde Jones.

Heidi found her table. It had a tent card with her name and Stanley's name in black curvy letters. There was also a white envelope with Heidi's name on it. *What's that?* she wondered. She set down the fishbowl. Dad placed a wooden stand on the middle of the table. Heidi covered the stand with a white scarf and set the bowl on top of it. She wanted her experiment to stand out, so her dad had helped her make a special stand.

"Looks great!" Dad said.

"Thanks," said Heidi.

Then she picked up the envelope

and turned away so no one would see what she was looking at. Inside the envelope she found a five-dollar gift card for Scoops ice-cream shop.

There was also a note:

> Here's the Scoop!
> I think you're cool!
>
> From,
> Your Secret Admirer

Heidi stuffed the note, gift card, and envelope in her backpack. When she looked up, Aunt Trudy winked at her. *Could Aunt Trudy be my secret admirer?* Heidi wondered.

She would have to find out later. Right now Heidi

needed to set up her science project. She and Dad went to the water fountain and filled the measuring cup with two quarts of water.

When they got back, Stanley had arrived with his portable music player and a sea-green poster. Fat paper letters

spelled DANCING RAISINS across the top. Stanley had drawn step-by-step pictures of how the science experiment worked. Note cards explained everything in words. He stood the poster on a stand beside the fishbowl.

"That looks amazing," said Heidi.

"So does the fishbowl," said Stanley.

Stanley and Heidi got to work. They had to get the raisins dancing by the time the judges got to the table.

Henry peered into the fishbowl. "I

wike the poo-poo wah-wah," he said with a mouthful of food. He really meant "I like the purple water."

"What are you eating?" asked Heidi.

Henry swallowed.

"Raisins," he said.

Heidi grabbed the box of raisins and looked inside. "OH NO!" she

shouted. “I can’t believe it! You just ate the most important part of our science experiment!”

Heidi grabbed her brother’s arm.

“Ow!” cried Henry. “What’s the big deal?”

Dad pulled Heidi and Henry apart.

“Settle down,” said Dad. “We can work this out.”

"But he ruined our experiment!" wailed Heidi.

"Hold on," said Aunt Trudy, putting her hand on Heidi's shoulder. "I have an idea."

Aunt Trudy pulled out a tin of gumballs from her purse. "I always keep gumballs on hand," she said. "They keep me from snacking."

Aunt Trudy chose a few sour-apple gumballs from the tin. "These feel just like mothballs," she explained. "The carbon dioxide bubbles can collect on their surfaces too. So they'll also work in your experiment."

Heidi stared at the lime-green gumballs.

"But our project is called 'Dancing Raisins,'" said Heidi. "Not 'Dancing Gumballs.'"

"I can fix that!" said Stanley. "I brought my art supplies just in case."

"You did?" said Heidi.

Stanley nodded.

Heidi let out a sigh of relief.

"You know what?" she said. "I'm glad we're partners."

"Me too," said Stanley.

KA-BOOM!

Plink!

Plink!

Plunk!

Heidi dropped the gumballs into the fishbowl. Stanley fixed the poster so it said DANCING GUMBALLS. Then he glued the word "gumballs" over the word "raisins" on all the note cards.

"I'm kind of glad that Henry ate the raisins," said Heidi.

"Me too," said Stanley. "Gumballs are cooler than raisins."

Henry ran up to the table. "The judges are walking around," he said.

Heidi spotted the judges at the first table.

"They won't get to us for a while," said Heidi. "Let's go look at the other experiments."

"Good idea," said Stanley.

Heidi and Stanley watched Lucy and Charlie show how a lemon battery works. They had five lemons with pennies, nails, and little cables attached to them. When they hooked up the cables to a tiny blue Christmas bulb, it lit up.

The judges clapped.

"Very well done!" said the mayor.

"I bet they'll win," said Heidi.

Stanley nodded.

Then they went to see Bruce and Melanie show off their volcano. The volcano sat on fake grass with mini plastic trees and houses all around it. Bruce was about to add the vinegar to the volcano when Melanie grabbed the bottle out of his hand.

"Let ME do it," said Melanie.

"Stop!" cried Bruce.

But it was too late.

Glug! Glug! Glug! Melanie poured half the bottle of vinegar into the volcano.

"Stand back!" shouted Bruce.

Everyone—except for Melanie—backed away from the table.

Ka-BOOM!

The volcano blew up. Melanie screamed as lava—which was really a stream of clay and bits of paper—splattered all over her face and clothes. A plastic tree hung from her long blond hair. Heidi, Lucy, and Bruce burst out laughing. Even Stanley laughed! Melanie clenched her fists and ran to the girls' bathroom.

"I'd say that was a huge success," said Bruce.

The judges frowned and wiped their sleeves.

POP
fiZZ
BOOGIE

DR. DESTRUCTO

Pop!

Fizz!

Boogie!

Stanley and Heidi's experiment was really in full swing once they were back at their table. The gumballs bounced up and down in the fishbowl.

"They're dancing like crazy!" said Stanley.

"Start the music!" said Heidi.

Stanley switched on the music player. The Charlie Brown theme song began to play. *Doo da doot doot, doo da doo . . . doo!*

"The gumballs look like they're really dancing to the music," said Heidi.

"It's magical," said Stanley.

"I agree," said the mayor, who had just arrived at their table.

The judges watched the gumballs dance to the music. They jotted some notes on their clipboards.

"What makes the gumballs dance?" asked the magazine editor.

"The music!" said Henry.

Everyone laughed. Then Heidi and Stanley took turns telling the judges what made the gumballs dance.

"Clever use of color," said the mayor.

"This is really great music," said

Principal Pennypacker as he snapped his fingers to the beat.

Then the judges moved on to the next table.

"Be right back," said Heidi.

Stanley nodded.

Heidi grabbed her backpack and raced to the water fountain. *Now's*

my chance to find out who my secret admirer is, she thought. She took the plastic bowl from her backpack and filled it with a cup of water. Then

she pushed open the door and stood in the hall. Heidi dropped a stick of gum in the bowl of water. Next she added two drops of the green food coloring and stirred it with a spoon. She put the bowl on the floor and stooped down next to it. Heidi pulled her medallion out from under her shirt and held it in her left hand. She placed her other hand over the mix and chanted the spell. The potion began to swizzle and swirl. Letters began to form in the fizzy green water.

Then—*wham!* The door to the gym banged into Heidi's back. She fell flat on her belly, and the potion spilled onto the floor before she could read the name.

"Ew, gross!" said someone behind her.

It was her brother, Henry.

"What are you drinking?" asked Henry. "Slime juice?"

Heidi jumped to her feet and grabbed her brother in a headlock.

Before she could really give it to him, the judges announced they had a winner. Heidi let go of Henry.

"Now come on, Dr. Destructo," said Heidi.

Heidi stuffed the bowl in her backpack and wiped up the mess with a paper towel.

Then they ran back inside.

I KNEW IT WAS YOU!

"Thank you, second graders of Brewster!" said the mayor. "We're so proud of each one of you." Everyone clapped. "This year's winning science project showed both hard work and imagination. Principal Pennypacker, would you please open the envelope?"

Principal Pennypacker pulled a piece of paper from the envelope.

"The winners of the second-grade science fair are . . . Heidi Heckelbeck and Stanley Stonewrecker!"

Everyone clapped and cheered.

Heidi squealed and Stanley pumped his fist in the air. Then they jumped up and down and hugged.

"I never even dreamed we'd win!" said Heidi.

"Well, *I* did!" said Stanley.

"Will the winners please come to the judges' table and accept your award?" asked Principal Pennypacker.

Heidi and Stanley made their way to the judges' table. Kids high-fived them and whistled as they walked by. The mayor put a medal around Heidi's neck, and then he put another one around Stanley's. The golden medal had three pictures: a beaker, a microscope, and the symbol of an atom.

Wow, thought Heidi as she and Stanley had their picture taken with the judges and Principal Pennypacker. *I've never won a medal before.* The excitement made her forget all about the ruined spell.

★ • ✱ ◎ •

"It was fun being partners," said Heidi as she and Stanley walked back to their table.

"Yeah, it sure was," said Stanley.

"And now the party's OVER," said Melanie, who still had crusty lava spattered all over her clothes. Melanie grabbed Stanley by the arm. "Come on, Stanley. Your weirdo duties are over, and I need help with my stuff."

"See ya," said Heidi.

"See ya," said Stanley.

When Heidi got back to the table, Dad, Mom, and Aunt Trudy had already packed everything up.

Bruce walked over and tapped Heidi on the shoulder. "Congratulations, Heidi," he said shyly. Then he handed something to her. "This is for you," he said. "It's a lava candy dispenser. It shoots Red Hots out of the top." It was Bruce's latest invention.

"Cool," said Heidi.

She pressed a button and a red candy popped out.

"I should've known you were my secret admirer all along," said Heidi.

Bruce looked puzzled, but before he could answer, his mother steered him toward the door.

"Your grandmother is waiting," said Bruce's mother.

They hurried off.

I'm sure Bruce is my admirer, thought Heidi. *Who else can it be?* She hugged her fishbowl and headed out the door with her family.

On the other side of the gym, Stanley Stonewrecker watched Heidi disappear behind the swinging doors.

"Don't tell me you *like* her?" said Melanie as she turned and walked toward the doors.

"Nah, of course not," said Stanley—with a smile.

Amy and the Missing Puppy

All of a sudden, Amy heard the jangle of a dog collar. Around the desk came a blur of brown and white fur. Amy felt a paw on either shoulder as she toppled off her chair. The next thing she knew, she was on the floor and a drooly Saint Bernard puppy was covering her face with doggy kisses.

Amy giggled and squealed. The Fitter Critter treats fell out of her pocket and scattered onto the floor. The puppy sniffed them before he gulped down three.

"Bad boy, Rufus! Naughty!" said Ms. Sullivan sternly. The puppy returned to Ms. Sullivan's side. He sat and looked up at her. His tail was wagging a mile a minute.

Still giggling, Amy picked herself up off the floor. She dried her face with the sleeve of her hoodie.

"Well, it looks like you've made a new friend," Ms. Sullivan said to Amy.

Amy looked up. For a split second, she thought she saw Ms. Sullivan's mouth turn up at the corners. Was that a *smile*? Amy had never seen Ms. Sullivan smile before. She'd never seen her with a puppy before either. *Huh*, she thought. *Ms. Sullivan doesn't seem like a pet person*.

Just then Amy's mother, Dr. Purvis came into the waiting room. "Hello, Marge! Hello, Rufus!" she said. She led them to an exam room.

Amy looked down at her favorite yellow hoodie. Below each shoulder was one perfect muddy paw print. *Guess Rufus found the wet flower bed on his way in!* Amy thought. She laughed and tried to wipe off the prints with a paper towel. It didn't help.

Rufus had left his mark.

Check out Heidi's
BOOK OF SPELLS BLOG
Book of Spells
and more!
at
heidiheckelbeck.com!